For my darling Bud – S.H.
To Lorna, Kaltoun, Penny and the
team at Macmillan for helping me bring
this book to the finish line– D.A.

First published 2022 by Macmillan Children's Books
an imprint of Pan Macmillan
The Smithson, 6 Briset Street, London, EC1M 5NR
EU representative: Macmillan Publishers Ireland Limited,
1st Floor, The Liffey Trust Centre, 117-126 Sheriff Street Upper,
Dublin 1, D01 YC43
Associated companies throughout the world
www.panmacmillan.com

ISBN (PB): 978-1-5290-1399-3
ISBN (Ebook): 978-1-5290-5213-8

Text copyright © Swapna Haddow 2022
Illustrations copyright © Dapo Adeola 2022

The rights of Swapna Haddow and Dapo Adeola to be identified as
the author and illustrator of this work have been asserted by them
in accordance with the Copyright, Designs and Patents Act 1988.

9 8 7 6 5 4 3 2 1

A CIP catalogue record for this book is
available from the British Library.

Printed in the UK

FSC
www.fsc.org

MIX
Paper from
responsible sources
FSC® C116313

Written by
SWAPNA HADDOW

Illustrated by
DAPO ADEOLA

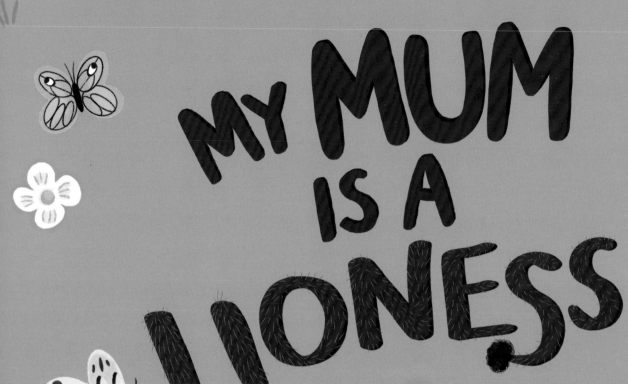

MY MUM IS A LIONESS

MACMILLAN CHILDREN'S BOOKS

Run!
HIDE!
My mum is a **lioness.**

She's been chasing
babies all day,

laying down her
catch on the floor.

And now she's
on the hunt for
bigger prey.

You can't outrun my mum.
She will catch you in a single **pounce**...

. . . because she is a mighty

lioness.

She spends all day thinking about how best to **serve** you up.

Perhaps you will be **tossed** in a wrap.

Perhaps you will be **seasoned.**
And perhaps you will be **roasted**
and **toasted** and drizzled in oil.

Because she is an imaginative **lioness.**

Sometimes she hunts in a pride.

No one is safe from the aunties.

Even Dad.

Even Grandad.

She always makes me show off for all the
aunties because she is a very proud **lioness.**

She paws at my hair and
pinches my cheeks.
And the Pride joins in too.

Mum loooooooves sports.

She teaches me how to chase

and how to pounce and how to leap
higher than all the other cubs.

Because she is a tireless **lioness**...

. . . But I'm still learning.

"MUM!"

She carries me to safety
and covers me in licks.

Her strong, warm **lioness HUGS** make everything better.

My mum might be a **lioness** but there isn't anyone I'd rather cuddle with than my mum. Besides, there are beasts fiercer than lionesses . . .

Wait until you see my little sister's

BITE!

One wild, stormy day, Bella opened her front
door and found a little stranger on her doorstep.

"Goodness!" she said. "You'd better come in before you get
blown away!" The little creature shivered and followed her
into the kitchen.

"Have a glass of water," said Bella. The little creature was **terribly** thirsty.

"Would you like some cornflakes and broccoli?" asked Bella. The little creature was **dreadfully** hungry too.

"Do you feel better now?" asked Bella. The little creature just **stared** up at her.

"You don't understand a word I'm saying, do you?" said Bella.

Mister
TOOTS

Emma Chichester Clark

HarperCollins Children's Books

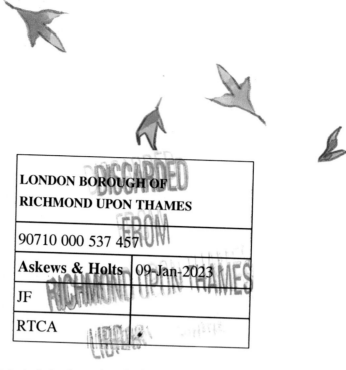

First published in hardback in the United Kingdom by HarperCollins *Children's Books* in 2022
This paperback edition published in 2023

HarperCollins *Children's Books* is a division of HarperCollins*Publishers* Ltd
1 London Bridge Street, London SE1 9GF

www.harpercollins.co.uk

HarperCollins*Publishers*
1st Floor, Watermarque Building, Ringsend Road,
Dublin 4, Ireland

1 3 5 7 9 10 8 6 4 2

ISBN 978-0-00-818033-1

Emma Chichester Clark asserts the moral right to be identified as the author and illustrator of the work.
A CIP catalogue record for this title is available from the British Library.

Printed and bound in Italy

This book is produced from independently certified FSC™ paper
to ensure resposnsible forest management.
For more information visit: www.harpercollins.co.uk/green

Just then, Tulip and Tadpole rushed in.

"Oh! Mummy!" cried Tadpole. "What is he? Can we keep him?"

"Well, I think he's lost," said Bella,
"and I don't think he speaks our language."

"Toot! Toot!"

cried the little creature, and waved his arms.

Toot! Toot!

Bella, Tulip and Tadpole took him up and down every street in town and asked everyone if they knew the little creature.

But nobody did. No one had ever seen him before.

"Poor little thing . . . all on his own," everyone said.

By the end of the day, Bella, Tulip and Tadpole still didn't know where the little creature had come from, but the little creature had learned to say "hello" and "goodbye" and "thank you".

When they got home, the little creature climbed on a chair and stared out of the window at the sky.

At bedtime, Tulip and Tadpole made him a comfy bed and kissed him goodnight.

But in the morning he was back
at the window **again**.

Tulip and Tadpole did everything they could to distract him
and cheer the little creature up . . .

and after a while . . .

he began to join in.

He learned to play lots of different games with Tulip
and Tadpole over the next day or two . . .

. . . but sometimes he looked **so sad,**
and he still often stared up at the sky.

"It's as if he's looking for someone
or something," said Tulip.

They wondered and worried about the little creature.
"We don't even know his name," sighed Tadpole.

"Let's call him **Mr Toots!**" said Bella.
"Because toot toot was the first thing he said to us."

Mr Toots beamed at Bella.

"He likes it!" said Tulip.

They **loved** him with all their hearts.

Everybody did.

The neighbours popped in to see him all the time . . .

and helped him settle in.

All the cousins and uncles and aunts **adored** him.

"He's the **sweetest** thing!"
said Aunt Esther.

"I wish we could take him home with us!" said
Rupert and Clarence.

"I wish he was mine!"
said Aunt Jemima.

But one day a terrible thing happened . . .

They went to the big park where there were lots of tall trees.

"Toot! Toot!"
cried Mr Toots,
and he began to run.

"Wait!" cried Tulip.
"Wait!" cried Tadpole.

But Mr Toots kept on running.

Bella watched with alarm . . .

. . . as he disappeared between the trees.

"Come on!" she cried.
"He can't have gone far!"

When they caught up with him, he was standing under a large chestnut tree. There was something hanging from the branches.

"Mine!" said Mr Toots.

Mine!

"I didn't know he knew that word," said Tulip.

"What is that thing?" asked Tadpole.

"It looks like a basket," said Bella.

Mr Toots jumped up and
started tugging at it.

Tulip grabbed his ankles and
Tadpole grabbed Tulip and Bella
hung on to Tadpole, and they
all pulled together.

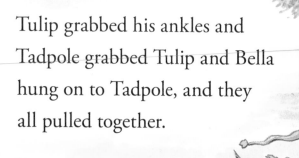

CRASH!

The basket suddenly came free.

Then, just as suddenly,
the wind picked up and
the basket began to fly away.

And Mr Toots jumped inside it!

WHOOSH!

"MR TOOTS!" cried Bella.

But the basket and Mr Toots were whooshed away in the wind.

Bella, Tulip and Tadpole ran as fast as they could, but they were TOO LATE . . .

Mr Toots was sailing,

up and up . . .

over the treetops.

Goodbye!

Goodbye! Thank you!

Mr Toots!

Mr Toots!

Mr Toots!

He was soon far out of sight.

"MUM!" wailed Tulip.

"MUM!" cried Tadpole.

"Oh, my darlings!" said Bella.
"I think our little Toots may be
going back to where he came from."

"I thought he'd stay
with us **forever**,"
said Tulip.

"I thought he **loved us**," said Tadpole.

At suppertime, none of them felt like eating.

At bedtime, Tulip said . . .
"I miss him **so much**
already."

"How can I sleep when I
don't know where he is?"
asked Tadpole.

Bella didn't sleep a wink either.

When friends and neighbours heard that Mr Toots
was missing they came to comfort them.

"Maybe he's happy where he's gone," said one.
"Perhaps you should try to forget him," said another.

And the days went by.

Soon it was a whole week
since Mr Toots had gone.

"I think he's **definitely**
forgotten us by now,"
said Tulip.

"We're **never** going
to see Mr Toots again,
are we?" said Tadpole.

Bella didn't know how to answer them.

Just then, there was a knock at the door . . .

. . . and there was
Mr Toots!

He grabbed Tadpole's paws.

"He wants us to follow him!" cried Tadpole.

"Come on, Mum!" cried Tulip. "Run!"

And as they ran they were joined by others . . .

More and **more**. Soon, the **whole** town was following Mr Toots.

Then, suddenly, everyone **stopped**.

They could **hardly believe their eyes.**

The sky was filled with baskets . . .

And the sound of little toots.

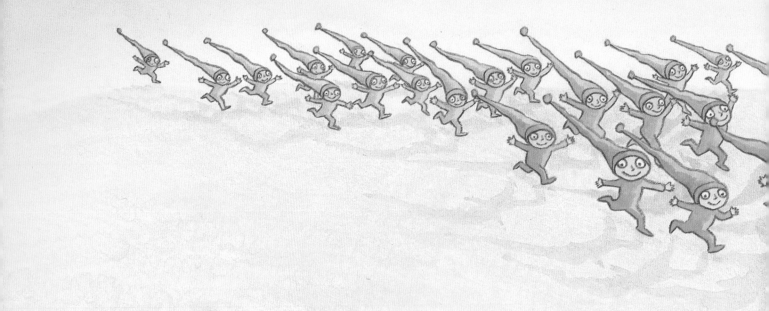

As the baskets landed, all the
little creatures jumped out of them
and ran towards the waiting crowd.

They were all given a warm welcome.

There was
someone for
everyone.

It **didn't matter** that they didn't speak the same language, because they all understood each other **perfectly.**

"So where would you like to go now, Mr Toots?" asked Bella.
"HOME!" said Toots.

"Forever?" whispered Tulip.

"Forever!" said Tadpole.

"And EVER!"
cried Mr Toots.